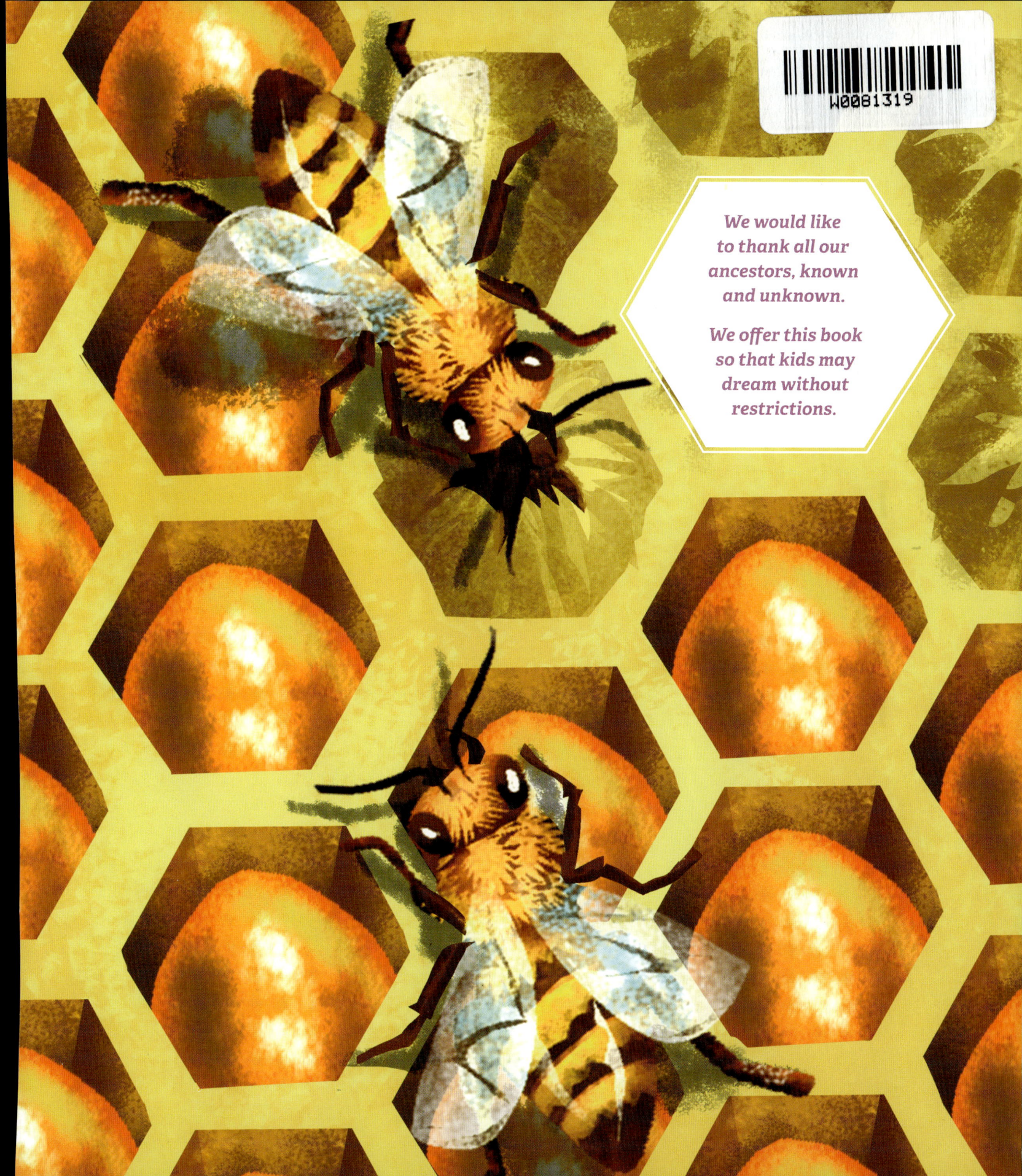

We would like
to thank all our
ancestors, known
and unknown.

We offer this book
so that kids may
dream without
restrictions.

AKEEM KEEPS BEES!

A Close-Up Look at the Honey Makers and Pollinators of Sankofa Farms

Kamal E. Bell, with Akeem Bell

Illustrations by Darnell Johnson

Storey Publishing

WELCOME TO SANKOFA FARMS!

Hi, I'm Akeem! My dad runs Sankofa Farms, so I spend a lot of time there. We do all sorts of cool things on the farm.

HELLO!

Welcome to our farm.

We use a big tractor to prepare the fields for planting.

We grow greens in the greenhouses year round!

Check out these baby lettuces!

We spread compost on the soil, which is like giving the plants vitamins to help them grow strong.

That watermelon is almost as big as you, Akeem!

In the fields we grow sweet, sun-ripened tomatoes and big, juicy watermelons!

How am I doing, Dad?

Great!

One of my favorite things that we do on the farm is raise honey bees!

I learn all about beekeeping from my dad, and I love teaching my friends about it, including you! With bees, there's something new to see and do in every season.

THE FiRST SPRiNG BEES

Bees spend most of the winter inside their hive. That's why springtime is so exciting—our bees finally leave their cozy home. When my dad first said I could help with the bees, I couldn't wait. I kept an eye and ear out for the first bees of the year.

When the weather warmed up and flowers started to bloom, the bees began to fly around the farm looking for pollen and nectar. I bet they were hungry!

Daddy, the bees are out!

We saw a bee with pollen on its legs. That's a good sign. If they're collecting pollen, that means there are new baby bees to feed.

The bees use pollen to make an important food called bee bread.

But not every bee colony makes it through winter. Wintertime can be tough for bees, especially if gets really cold or the bees don't have enough honey to eat.

This hive is quiet. I don't think they made it.

I know, it's sad. But that hive won't be quiet for long. We'll be getting new bees in just a few weeks, and you can help me move them into their new home.

Hurray!

A BEE IS BORN

Honey bees don't start out their lives looking like bees at all. They go through some big changes called metamorphosis—like butterflies!

Spring is when the queen bee starts laying eggs again. Each egg gets its own cell in the comb, like a tiny bee nest.

Eat up and grow big and strong!

Then the eggs hatch into baby bees called larvae or grubs. Their main job is to eat and grow. At first, the grubs don't look like bees at all. But just wait!

After five or six days, worker bees use wax to seal the larvae inside the cells. This is when the larvae transform into the next stage: pupae.

Sleep tight!

From Larva to Pupa

Larvae look like little white grubs. The larva spins a cocoon around itself and begins to pupate, growing eyes, legs, wings, and fuzzy hair.

Thirteen days later, the pupa has changed into an adult bee and chews its way through the wax.

Happy Bee-day!

A PACKAGE ARRIVES

Did you know that bees can be shipped in the mail? When our new bees arrived, they came in a wooden box with a screen so they could breathe fresh air. In the box there were 3 pounds of worker bees and a can of sugar water. My dad said 3 pounds is about 10,000 bees! Whoa, that's a lot of bees.

Inside the big box, there was also a very small box with a screen.

And what's in that tiny box?

This is the queen bee. We have to introduce her to the other bees in a special way.

Each queen bee has a scent made by chemicals called pheromones. The worker bees need to get used to their new queen's scent before they'll accept her into the colony—otherwise they'll think she's an intruder and attack her!

Yummm... candy...

Hey, who's that?

Do I know you?

The queen bee's box was sealed at one end with a plug made from sugar.

It takes a little while, but the worker bees will eat this candy plug to reach the queen. By then, they'll be used to having her around.

WHAT WE WEAR

We waited for a warm spring day to introduce the bees to their new home. But first we had to get ready! Even though we do our best to keep the bees calm, we still need to protect ourselves from stings, just in case. This is my bee suit. It's funny-looking, but it's important!

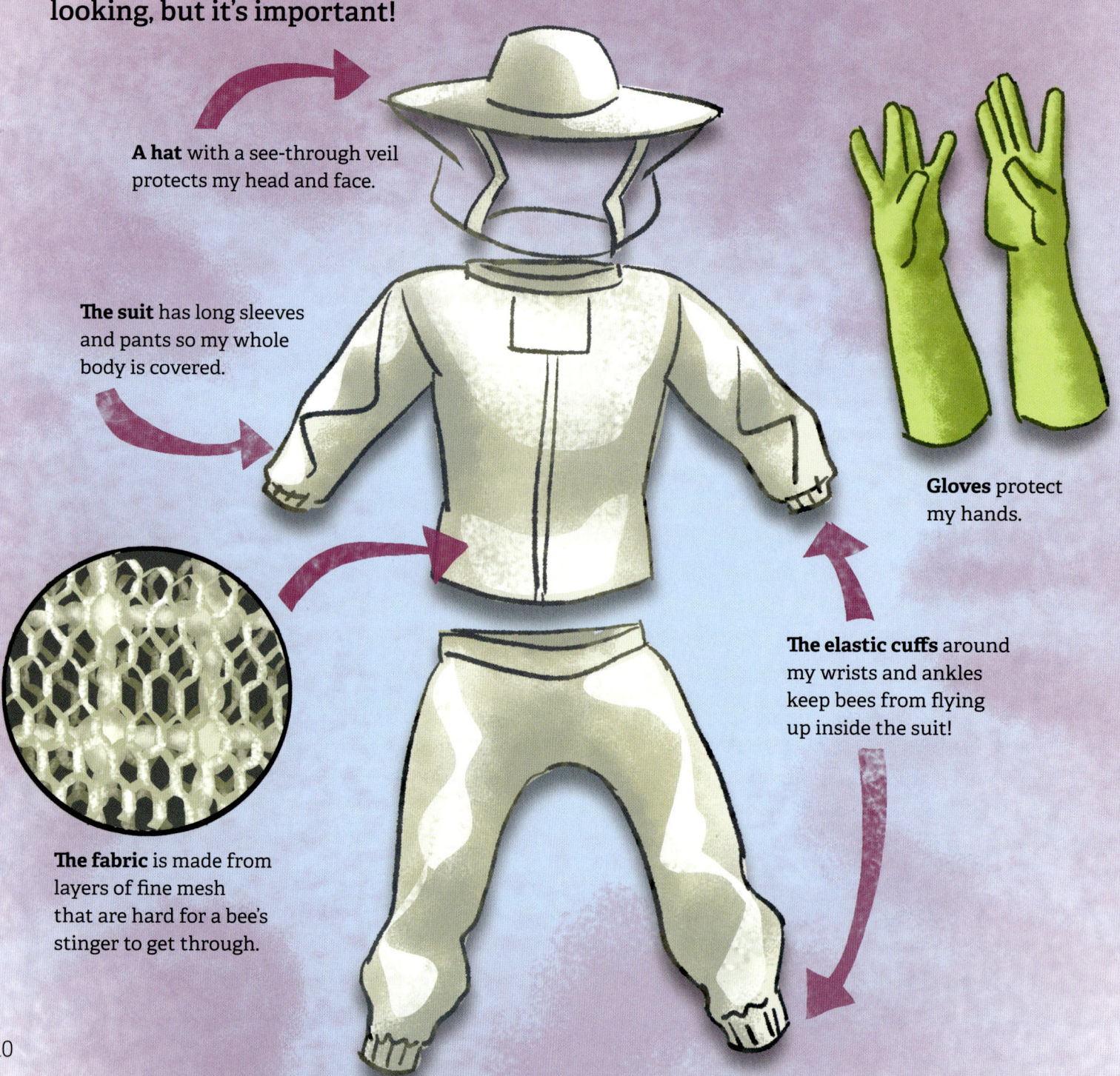

A hat with a see-through veil protects my head and face.

The suit has long sleeves and pants so my whole body is covered.

Gloves protect my hands.

The elastic cuffs around my wrists and ankles keep bees from flying up inside the suit!

The fabric is made from layers of fine mesh that are hard for a bee's stinger to get through.

TOOLS

Along with our bee suits, we have some special tools for beekeeping, too.

The bee brush has long, soft bristles for gently sweeping the bees out of the way when it's time to collect honey.

The hive tool is super helpful for opening the hive and lifting frames, especially when they are really sticky!

This is a smoker. A few puffs of smoke can make the bees calmer and easier to work with. My dad stuffs the smoker with some dry grass and leaves and lights it with a match to get it going.

Scent is one of the main ways bees "talk" to one another. When bees sense danger, they use scent to send messages that tell the other bees to attack. The smoke interrupts these messages, so the bees stay calm.

Squeeze the bellows like this so the smoke puffs out the top.

Hey! I think—

...Did you say something?

MOVING IN

Finally, we were ready. It was time to put the package of bees into a hive!
The bees won't just fly into their new home, though. We had to give them
a little help on move-in day.

THE BEES' NEW HOME

Here's a tour of a typical beehive, where the bees live, raise their babies, and (hopefully!) make lots of honey.

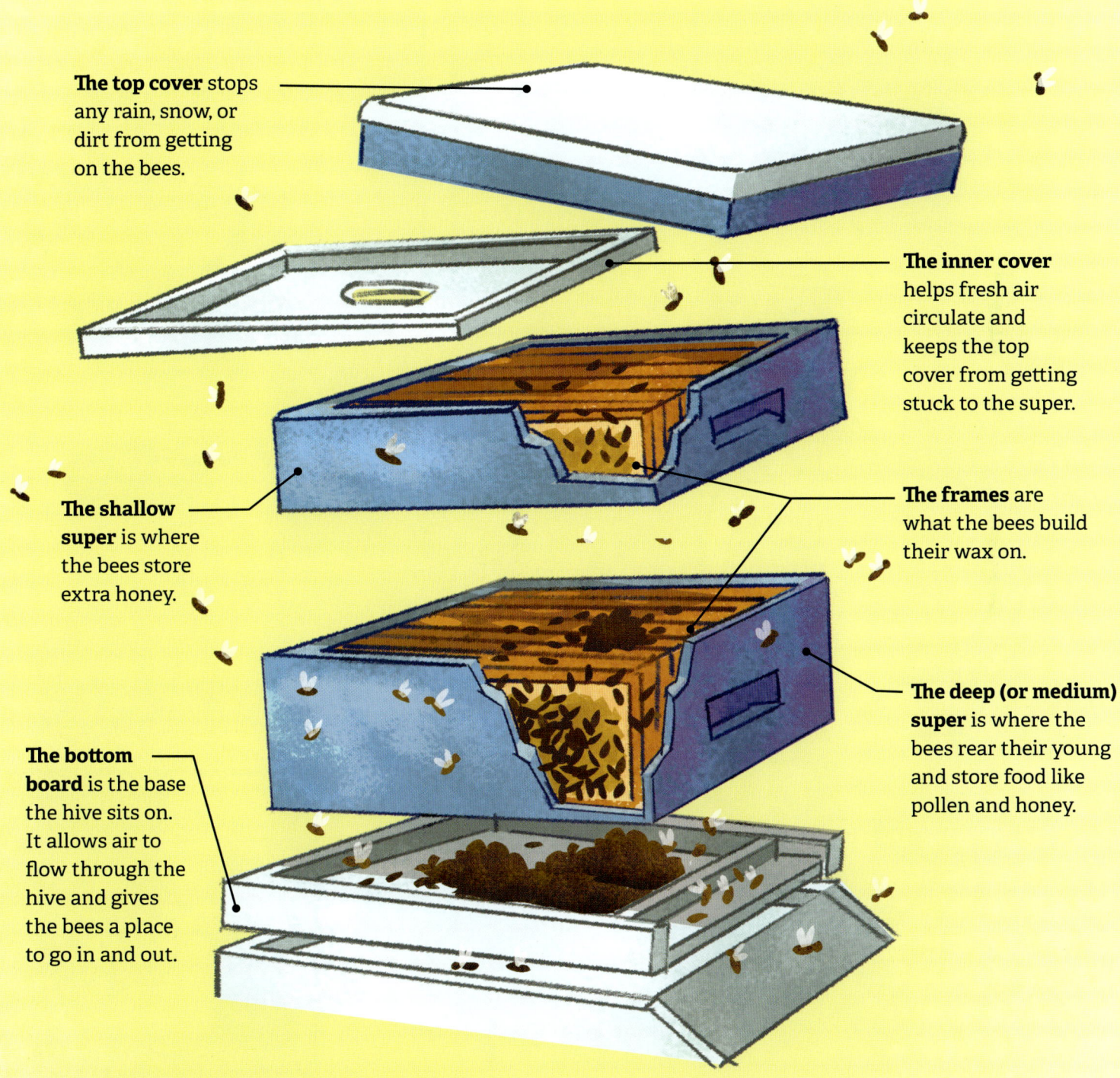

The top cover stops any rain, snow, or dirt from getting on the bees.

The inner cover helps fresh air circulate and keeps the top cover from getting stuck to the super.

The shallow super is where the bees store extra honey.

The frames are what the bees build their wax on.

The bottom board is the base the hive sits on. It allows air to flow through the hive and gives the bees a place to go in and out.

The deep (or medium) super is where the bees rear their young and store food like pollen and honey.

BUSY BEES

Three basic types of bees came in our package. Why? Well, turns out they each have a special role to play. They got right to work in their new home.

Most of the 10,000 bees in the package were **worker bees**.

The **worker bees** are female and do all the work to run the hive. They are always busy.

So most of the bees in here are girls! What do they all do?

The worker bees clean and protect the colony, take care of the baby bees, collect nectar and pollen, make wax, and make honey.

Wow.

Golden honey made here!

Here's some fresh wax to cap that cell.

Have some food, baby bee...

Gotta clean up!

Thanks!

The **drones** are male, but there are a lot fewer of them.

The **drones** have one job to do. They mate with the queen on her mating flight, giving her the last ingredient she needs to make her eggs hatch into baby bees.

The **queen bee** is a female like the workers.

The **queen bee**'s main job is to lay eggs. She lays thousands of eggs a day during the spring and summer.

THE BEES HELP THE FARM

As soon as the bees settled into their new home, they started exploring the farm. I saw them zooming around all the time! Flying might look like fun, but these bees were doing important work.

Honey bees visit flowers to collect nectar and pollen so they can make bee bread and honey to eat. As bees buzz from flower to flower, they spread pollen around so the plants can make fruit and seeds. This is called pollination.

Many plants on our farm need bees to help with pollination.

So we wouldn't have food like melons and squash without their help!

Did you know bees have two stomachs? When bees drink flower nectar, most of it goes into their "honey stomach" so they can start turning it into honey and carry it back to the hive.

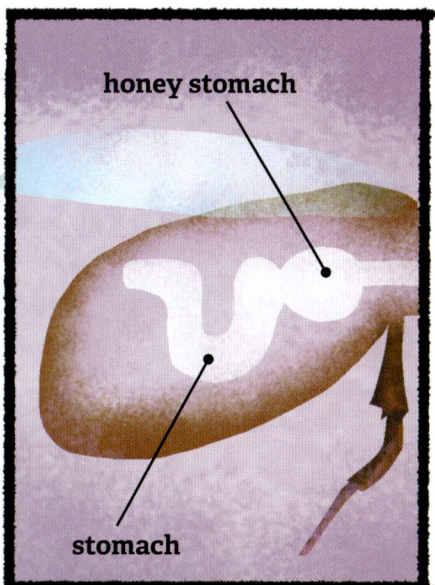

Bees collect flower pollen, too. The pollen sticks to the hairs on the bee's body.

The bee shapes the pollen into pellets . . .

. . . and attaches them to its hind legs.

But collecting pollen is messy work. The bee ends up scattering pollen everywhere . . .

. . . and accidentally carries some of that pollen to other plants that need it!

HOW HONEY IS MADE

Once a bee has a full load of nectar or pollen, it heads back to the hive where other bees are busy making honeycomb and honey. These younger worker bees are called "house" bees.

As bees arrive from the outside, they pass their nectar from their honey stomach to the house bees, mouth to mouth.

The bees fill each cell in the comb with nectar and pollen.

Next, the bees crawl around the comb, fluttering their wings like fans. This breeze thickens the nectar mixture into honey.

Once the honey is ready, worker bees put a wax lid on each cell to store the honey until it's needed.

HOW BEES BUILD HONEYCOMB

But bees don't just make honey—they make honeycomb, too!

Before bees collect any nectar or pollen, they need a place to store it. That's what comb is for.

Bees have a gland that turns the honey they eat into wax flakes that form on their bodies. The bees chew the wax like gum to make it softer.

Can I have a piece?

Working together, the bees form the soft wax into tubes that are six-sided, or hexagonal. These tubes are for honey storage. In a different part of the hive, bees build more comb so the queen has a place to lay her eggs.

19

FEEDING THE BEES

Did you know bees can run out of food? We checked on our new hive a lot, but it didn't seem to have much honey in it. My dad told me it was time to help our bees by feeding them!

Honey is the best food for bees, but since we didn't have any stored honey left over from other colonies, the best thing to do was to feed the bees sugar water.

Where is the honey?

This is where the bees store their honey, but since there isn't much, we will have to feed these bees to help them out.

Here's how we made the sugar water: We got an empty bucket, a bag of pure cane sugar, a jar, and some warm water.

SUGAR

First, we filled the jar with sugar and dumped it into the bucket.

Then we filled the jar with warm water and dumped it in, too.

Finally, we mixed them together until the sugar dissolved.

That's it!

Let's go feed the bees!

We took the top cover off the hive and added a container called a top feeder. Then we poured the sugar water into the feeder.

This will give the bees some energy until they can make enough honey to feed themselves.

THE HONEY IS FLOWING

Every week or so, we inspected the hives to see how the bees were doing. By late spring, everything was in bloom at the farm. The plants were making lots of nectar and pollen, so the bees were busy gathering it!

Sometimes bees make more honey than their hive can hold. That's a problem because then they won't have room to raise more baby bees or store more honey.

We're running out of room! Now what?

Maybe we should move?

To keep this from happening, we had to make the hive bigger. We did this by adding another box of frames, called a super, on top of the hive.

If there is enough honey and bees, we can also give the bees more room by splitting the colony into two separate hives.

What happens if we aren't careful and the bees run out of room?

Oh no!

Some of the bees will leave to start a new colony somewhere else.

SWARM!

A huge swarm of buzzing honey bees might look a little scary, but most of the time, it's just a colony looking for a new home.

If a bee colony gets too big for its hive, half the worker bees and their queen rush out in a big cloud. This is called swarming.

The swarm surrounds the queen and waits somewhere while a few of the bees look for a new place to live. Once these "scouts" find somewhere to build a hive, the swarm will move in.

We go where she goes!

Stay near our queen!

Hey, I found an amazing new house!

Let's check it out!

What about the bees that stay behind in the old hive? Their queen is gone!

Don't worry, those bees were thinking ahead. A new queen will soon be born from one of the colony's eggs.

You're right. That's why we make the hives bigger or split colonies to give them more room in their hives.

But we don't want our bees to move away!

TIME FOR A HONEY HARVEST

It takes weeks and a lot of nectar for bees to make honey. The more flowers that are in bloom, the more honey the bees can make. Honey is ready to harvest when the hive has frames that are full of capped honey.

We used a hive tool to pry each frame from the super.

Each frame was full of bees—and honey!

We've outdone ourselves!

Good work, sisters.

We used our handy bee brush to gently sweep the bees off the frame.

When each frame was bee-free, we put it in a bin.

Then we carried the frames indoors.

IS THE HONEY . . . STUCK?

Once we had the frames out, I wondered how we were going to get all that honey out of the comb! One way is to use a machine called a honey extractor. The honey extractor looks like a big metal drum.

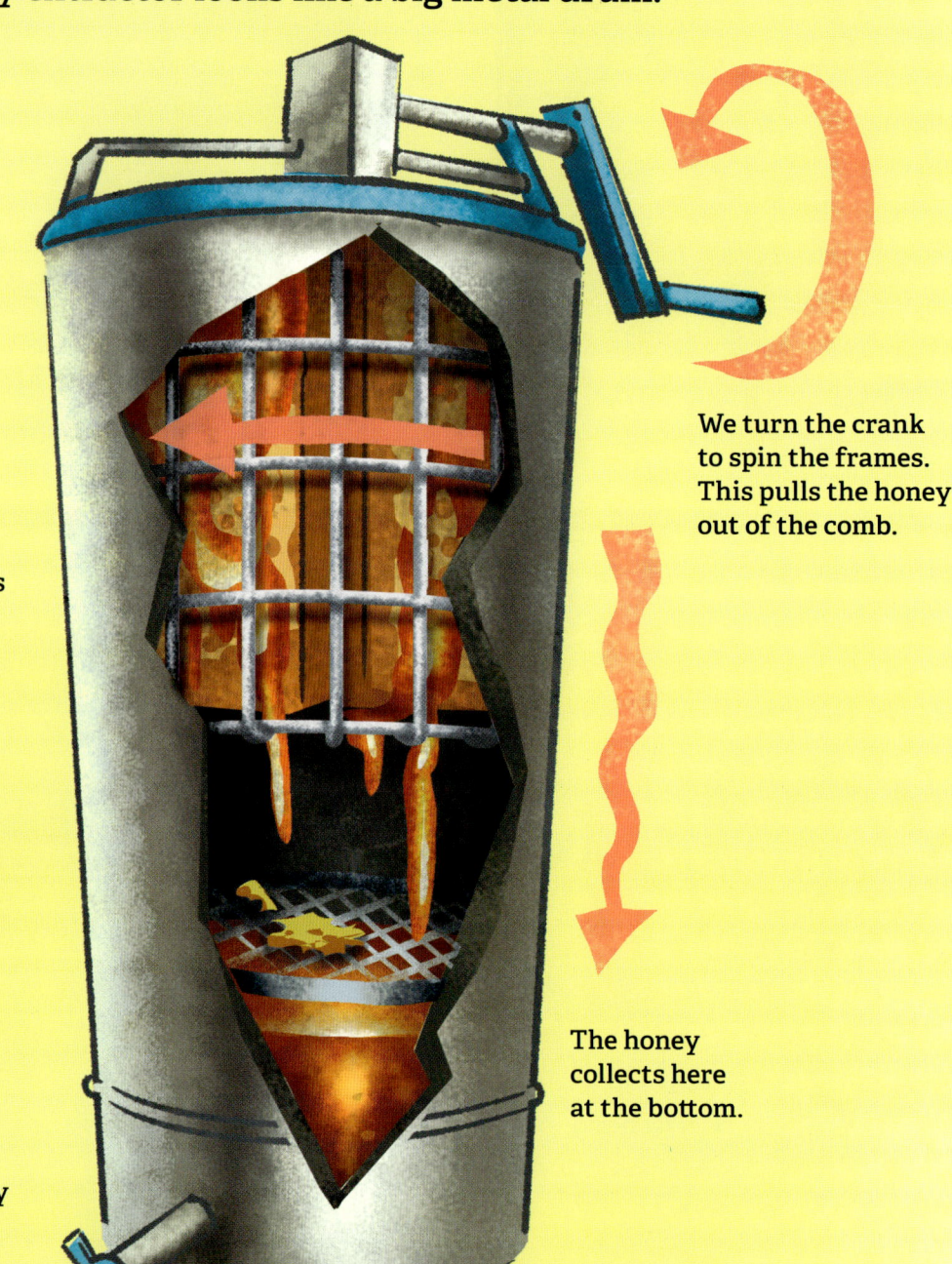

We turn the crank to spin the frames. This pulls the honey out of the comb.

Several frames can fit inside the extractor.

This one has a built-in strainer that catches any pieces of wax.

The honey collects here at the bottom.

We open the honey gate to pour our honey into jars!

We took the frames out of the bin one at a time. My dad used a knife to slice off the wax caps from the honeycomb.

Look at all that honey!

We turned the extractor's crank to spin the frames really fast.

I'm cranking as fast as I can!

Once all the honey had dripped to the bottom, we opened the spout and filled jars with honey!

Isn't that beautiful?

It looks like gold . . .

There's nothing like a snack of honey from your very own bees!

MMMM

NOT ENOUGH TO GO AROUND

In late summer, the weather became hot and dry and there weren't as many flowers blooming. That meant less food for bees.

When there are fewer flowers blooming, the bees stop expanding their colony. My dad says this is called dearth.

Whew! I had to go a long way to find some flowers.

There just aren't as many out there!

So many mouths to feed! I better stop laying so many eggs.

When we inspected the bees, we saw something strange.

Dad, are those bees fighting?

We had left plenty of honey for the bees in this hive, but a neighboring colony was trying to steal it. Beekeepers call this "robbing."

Get out of here!

We're hungry! I know you have food in there!

One way to help the bees defend themselves from robbing is to use something called an entrance reducer.

How is that going to help?

It makes the hive entrance smaller so the bees can guard it more easily.

Good thing the doorway isn't so big anymore.

Hey! Stay away!

31

MITES!

One day, I saw a weird red dot on a bee! I thought the bee was hurt.

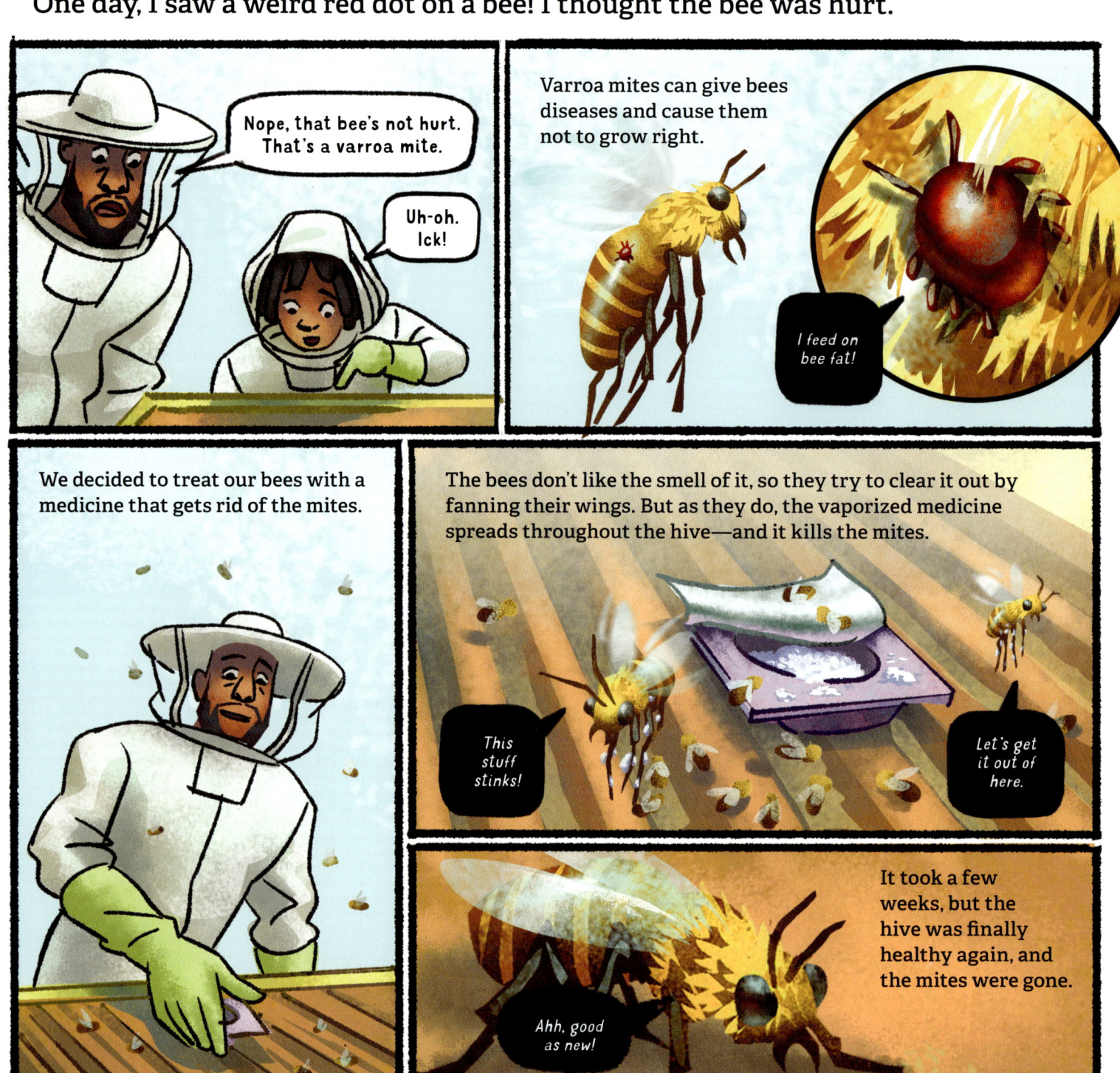

Nope, that bee's not hurt. That's a varroa mite.

Uh-oh. Ick!

Varroa mites can give bees diseases and cause them not to grow right.

I feed on bee fat!

We decided to treat our bees with a medicine that gets rid of the mites.

The bees don't like the smell of it, so they try to clear it out by fanning their wings. But as they do, the vaporized medicine spreads throughout the hive—and it kills the mites.

This stuff stinks!

Let's get it out of here.

It took a few weeks, but the hive was finally healthy again, and the mites were gone.

Ahh, good as new!

BEARDING

One day it was so hot, all I wanted to do was go swimming, but it was time to check the hives. A big clump of bees was hanging off the outside of a hive! Turns out this is called bearding. It looked like the hive had grown a bee beard!

High temperatures can be dangerous for bee babies, so it's important to keep the hive from getting too hot. With fewer bees inside the hive, there's more room for air to flow.

These adult bees were hanging around outside the hive so that the inside could cool off.

Whew! Was it hot in there or was it just me?

Definitely not just you!

Another way bees keep their hive cool is by fanning their wings outside the hive entrance.

All fans on deck!

Get that air moving!

COMBINING HIVES

In the fall, the weather started to cool off. The bees had to work harder to find food because there were even fewer flowers. When we went to check on the bees, it seemed like there weren't as many as before.

Dad, I think this bee colony got smaller.

Will they be okay?

Well, it is harder for small hives to survive the winter. But there's something we can do to help.

One big hive has a better chance of surviving than two little ones, so my dad showed me how we can combine them. You have to make sure to do it on a warm day.

First, we took the top off one hive and spread newspaper over the open super.

Then we set the second hive on top of the first hive with the newspaper in between them.

Won't the bees fight?

Nope. Give them a few days and see what happens!

Dad was right. It was amazing! The bees could smell each other through the paper and got used to each other's scent.

When we went back to check on them a few days later, the bees had chewed through the newspaper to become one hive.

Hey, nice to meet you!

My house is your house!

The worker bees picked the strongest of the two queens and kept her. The other queen got chased out!

So long!

THE FARM IN WINTER

When winter arrived, everything on the farm slowed down—especially the bees.

WINTER BEES

The queen is the longest-living bee in a colony. Queen bees can live for up to five years. Workers live only six weeks or so, and drones live just a week or two longer. But before winter arrives, a special generation of female bees is born that can live for up to six months! These "winter bees" are the superheroes of the colony.

Unlike the larvae born in the summer, these baby bees aren't fed very much protein in their diet.

They grow a layer of tissue, sort of like fat, which makes them bigger than other workers. It also creates a chemical that helps the bees live longer and stay healthier. Talk about superpowers!

When it gets colder than 50 degrees outside, the winter bees stay inside the hive and huddle together in a big cluster. They shiver to create heat and crawl together in a group to reach their stored honey. The queen is in the center of the cluster where it's extra warm.

SPRiNG RETURNS

After a few months, winter will change to spring. The queen will begin laying eggs again, and the winter bees will begin collecting fresh nectar and pollen to feed the next generation of bees.

As the bees begin to buzz again, our farm will wake up for a new year of planting, growing, and beekeeping.

SANKOFA FARMS

Sankofa Farms is a real place!

Akeem's dad, **Kamal Bell**, grew up in Durham, North Carolina, where he saw for himself that good, healthy food wasn't easy to come by if you lived in certain communities. In college, he learned about "food deserts" and how healthy food wasn't accessible to everyone, usually because of their socio-economic status. He decided to do something about it—and that is how Sankofa Farms was born.

The goal of Sankofa Farms is to create a sustainable food source for people in both rural and urban areas of Durham and Orange County, North Carolina. The Sankofa Farms Agricultural Academy helps young men learn STEM skills that can be used on the farm—including beekeeping. They partner with community organizations to take food from the farms to the tables of people who need it most.

Khalil, this watermelon's heavy!

Because everyone deserves farm-fresh healthy food!

Good thing we're so strong, Akeem!

We love to serve our community!

Thanks for your help, Khalil!

Look at all this fennel!

Sankofa is a family farm, and the whole family helps out. Akeem has an older brother named Khalil and a younger brother named Adé. His mom, Amber, helps on the farm, too.

Akeem got interested in beekeeping one day when he saw his dad inspecting the hives. The first time he learned to recognize the queen, he got really excited and has not stopped asking about the bees since.

Is the smoker ready?

Yep. Are you ready to visit the bees?

It's not a space suit—it's a bee suit!

It's important to wear protective gear when working with the bees. They even make kid-size bee suits!

We check on the hives regularly to make sure they are healthy.

Let's have a look at these frames.

A frame full of bees is a sign of a healthy colony!

Every year hundreds of people come to Sankofa Farms to learn about working with honey bees. The farm makes around 200 pounds of honey a year and gives it away to people in the community. There's nothing like the sweet taste of honey made by local bees!

A BEEKEEPER'S GLOSSARY

bearding When a clump of bees hangs on to the outside of the hive on a hot day, allowing the inside of the hive to cool off.

bee bread A food made out of pollen that bees make to feed their young. Nurse bees also need to eat bee bread to produce brood jelly, which is fed to the larvae.

bee brush A soft tool for brushing bees out of the way when collecting honey.

cells The six-sided (hexagonal) wax tubes that make up the comb.

comb The basic structure of the beehive, made of many cells side by side. Bees store nectar, pollen, and honey in the comb, and also raise their young here.

dearth When a bee colony stops expanding because of lack of food.

drone A male bee.

frame What the bees build their wax comb on.

hive tool A specially shaped bar for prying open the hive and lifting the frames.

honey The thick, sweet substance made by bees from the nectar of flowers.

honey extractor A machine for getting honey out of the comb.

honey stomach Where bees store nectar inside their bodies so they can bring it back to the hive. Not their true stomach.

larva A white grub that hatches from an egg and goes on to become a pupa and then an adult bee. Plural: larvae

metamorphosis A process of multiple stages in which a bee (or other insect) changes from an immature form to an adult.

nectar A sugary liquid made by flowers to attract pollinators such as bees.

pheromone A unique scent made by chemicals in an animal's body, used to send signals to others.

pollen Powdery grains made by flowers so that the plants can reproduce by pollination.

pollination The process of transferring pollen from the male part of a flower to a female part. This allows plants to make fruits and seeds.

pupa The stage of a bee's life just before it emerges as an adult. The pupa is sealed inside a cell and spins a cocoon around itself. Plural: pupae

queen A female bee whose job it is to lay eggs. The largest bee in the colony.

robbing When one bee colony steals food from another.

scout A worker bee who looks for a new place for her colony to live.

smoker A tool for puffing smoke into a hive to calm the bees.

super A hive box containing the comb where the bees store honey.

swarm A colony of bees looking for a new home.

top cover A lid to keep rain, snow, and dirt from getting into the beehive.

varroa mite A parasite that can give bees diseases and cause them not to grow right.

winter bees A special generation of female bees born in late fall that can live for up to six months.

worker bees Female bees who do various jobs to run the hive.

INDEX

The mission of Storey Publishing is to serve our customers by
publishing practical information that encourages
personal independence in harmony with the environment.

Edited by Deborah Burns and Hannah Fries

Art direction and book design by Jessica Armstrong

Text production by Jennifer Jepson Smith

Photography by Devin McAllister, 40 l., 41–43;
    Cornell Watson, 40 r.

Illustrations by © Darnell Johnson

Storey books may be purchased in bulk for business,
educational, or promotional use. Special editions or book
excerpts can also be created to specification. For details,
please contact your local bookseller or the Hachette Book
Group Special Markets Department at special.markets@
hbgusa.com.

Storey Publishing
210 MASS MoCA Way
North Adams, MA 01247
storey.com

Storey Publishing is an imprint of Workman
Publishing, a division of Hachette Book Group, Inc.,
1290 Avenue of the Americas, New York, NY 10104.
The Storey Publishing name and logo are registered
trademarks of Hachette Book Group, Inc.

Distributed in Europe by Hachette Livre, 58 rue
Jean Bleuzen, 92 178 Vanves Cedex, France

Distributed in the United Kingdom by Hachette
Book Group, UK, Carmelite House, 50 Victoria
Embankment, London EC4Y 0DZ

ISBNs: 978-1-63586-609-4 (paper over board);
978-1-63586-610-0 (ebook)

Printed in Humen Town, Dongguan, China by R. R. Donnelley
on paper from responsible sources

10   9   8   7   6   5   4   3   2   1

APS

Library of Congress Cataloging-in-Publication Data on file